Star Girl is first published in the United States in 2015
by Picture Window Books
A Capstone imprint
1710 Roe Crest Drive
North Mankato, Minnesota 56003
www.capstonepub.com

Library of Congress Cataloging-in-Publication Data is available on the Library of
Congress website.

ISBN: 978-1-4795-8278-5 (library binding)
ISBN: 978-1-4795-8282-2 (paperback)
ISBN: 978-1-4795-8474-1 (eBook PDF)

Summary: Planet Rednessis has been plunged into total darkness, and the reptaliens
are turning on each other. When Space Cadet Star Girl and her two besties investigate,
they learn that being kept in the dark can be disastrous. Can the cadets sort themselves
out in time to save both the planet and its inhabitants?

Designer: Natascha Lenz

This *Three's A Crowd* US Edition is published by arrangement with Macmillan
Education Australia Pty Ltd, 15 - 19 Claremont Street, South Yarra, Vic 3141,
Australia

Printed in the United States of America by Corporate Graphics

STAR ★ GIRL

SAVING SPACE ONE PLANET AT A TIME

THREE'S A CROWD

LOUISE PARK

PICTURE WINDOW BOOKS
a capstone imprint

SPACE EDUCATION

Protective Dome

Boys' Dorm

Horse Riding Club

Dome Traveler

Space Tube

Repair Center

Classrooms

Stabilizer Units

FlyBy

Spaceball Court

Docking Bays

The Comet Café

Celebration Holopods

Movie Theater and Bowling Hub

Energy Core

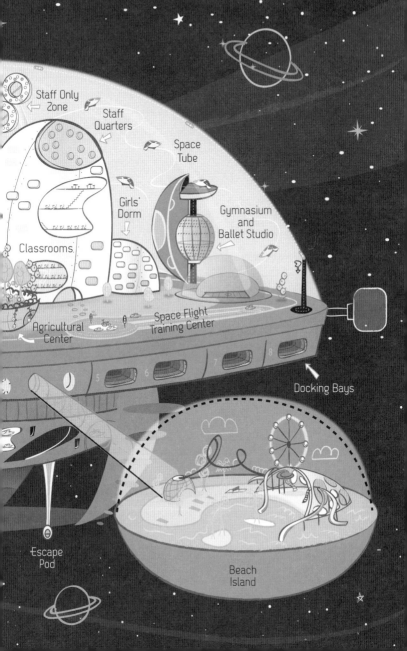

ND **ACTION SCHOOL**

Staff Only Zone

Staff Quarters

Space Tube

Girls' Dorm

Gymnasium and Ballet Studio

Classrooms

Agricultural Center

Space Flight Training Center

Docking Bays

Escape Pod

Beach Island

SEAS

A SPACE STATION BOARDING SCHOOL FOR GIRLS AND BOYS

The Space Education and Action School is located on Space Station Edumax. Students in the space training program complete space missions on planets in outer space that are in danger and need help.

Not all students will make it through to their final year and only the best students will go on to become space agents. Addie must make it through and become a Space Agent. Outer space needs her.

CONFIDENTIAL
STAFF ONLY

Program: Space Cadetship

Student: Adelaide Banks

Space Cadet: Star Girl

Age: 10 years old

School house: Stellar

Space missions: 3

Earned mission points: 26

Earned house points: 110

Comments: Adelaide is beginning to show the makings of a good space cadet. However, she continues to have some friendship problems. This may be affecting her performance on missions and in class. All staff need to help her through this bumpy settling-in period.

CHAPTER ⭐ ONE

"Your first birthday at the school, Ads!" said Miya. "It'll be tons of fun."

"It'll be different, that's for sure," said Addie looking around the celebration holopod.

Addie, Olivia, and Miya were all standing in the main celebration holopod.

"What theme are you going to pick?" asked Olivia. "You can create any world or environment you want with this holographic equipment. It's *so* cool. You can make different skies and settings with just a click of the pod's party programmer."

"There's so much here," answered Addie, looking down at the party folder Ms. Bradstock had given her. "I've never seen anything like this place. I don't know what to pick for the food or the activities or anything."

"Just do one thing at a time, then," said Miya. "Let's pick a theme and create the world first. You can choose the rest after."

There were fairy kingdoms, dinosaur adventures, jungle safaris, undersea worlds, pirate themes, magic themes, rock star themes, and tons more. The list was endless.

"Okay, good plan, Miya," said Addie.

Olivia frowned. "That's what *I* just asked

you to do—pick a theme," she said to Addie. "I may as well not even be here!"

"Hey, I didn't ignore you, Olivia," said Addie. "You asked what theme I was going to pick, and Miya suggested how I should go about it." Addie could see Olivia was still annoyed. "I'm just a little blown away by all this," she tried to explain. "You've been in the celebration pods before. I haven't. Anyway, I think it will be easier if I go with the activities first. Dad said nothing really expensive."

"What about the super-silver-jewelry-making-moments party?" Olivia suggested. "I'd love to do that."

"That's one of the most expensive parties you can have," Miya pointed out.

"Whatever! I'm going to go and look at the karaoke stuff," Olivia said, and she stomped off.

"What's with her lately?" asked Addie.

"What do you mean?" asked Miya as she looked through the party folder.

"She's been kind of weird ever since you and I came back from our last mission."

"Kind of weird?"

"Like, she has to be with me all the time," said Addie. "And just then, how she thought I didn't listen to her. That sort of stuff."

"Yeah, you're right. She has been a little weird," said Miya. "Let's just get your party done, then we'll deal with her. Hey, what about a mini-makeover party or the pop star party? They'd be tons of fun."

"Or what about the supermodel one?" Addie asked as she touched the supermodel icon on the party programmer. Suddenly the room was transformed. A fully lit modeling catwalk appeared on the holopod floor and it went down the center of the room. Bright spotlights crisscrossed over the catwalk and the dome roof was covered with stars.

"How awesome is this?" Addie asked. "I love it! Look at these clothes and those cool beds. I can't wait to have a sleepover here."

"And it won't cost much at all," said Miya. "The disco and karaoke are free. And we can all bring our own makeup, nail polish, hair straighteners, and other stuff to use."

"We can do each other's hair and makeup and put on a show. Then go into the disco for a karaoke night. What do you think, Olivia?" Addie asked, trying to pull her friend back into the party fun.

"Yep, it would be awesome," said Olivia, looking over the new karaoke list.

Just then the door of the pod opened and Ms. Bradstock walked in with a group of girls.

"What an exciting choice, Addie," Ms. Bradstock said as she looked around the pod. "Is this the theme you've chosen?"

"I think so," Addie replied. "Is this pod still free for my birthday?"

"Well, the main pod is kept for large parties. Your party is for twelve girls, right?"

"Yes, that's right," said Addie, and then she saw Valentina among the group of girls. *Oh no,* she thought. *I forgot—we share the same birthday.* "Hi, Valentina," she said. "Are you planning to celebrate your birthday on Saturday night too?"

"Yes," said Valentina. "It will be the party of the year. I'll need this main pod to fit all the people I'm inviting."

"Oh, what kind of party are you going to have?" Olivia asked.

"The super-silver-jewelry-making-moments," answered Valentina.

"Addie, Celebration Pod 2 is the perfect size for your group," said Ms. Bradstock. "Come with me and I'll show it to you. You can still have everything you see here. All the holopods can create all the party themes."

"Oh, okay," answered Addie, trying not to sound disappointed. "I'll just get my bag and head over."

As Addie went to collect her things, Olivia raced over to Valentina. "I love the sound of that jewelry-making party," she said to her.

"Yeah, and that's just the first thing. I'll also have tons of other activities," said Valentina. She smirked. "But nothing as lame as a supermodel party."

"Oh, good," agreed Olivia. "A supermodel party would be so boring."

"Olivia," Miya snapped. "What's with you? You just told Addie it would be fun."

But Addie didn't stay to hear Olivia's reply. She ran out of the pod.

"Do you even care that you hurt her feelings?" asked Miya as she watched Addie leave. "I don't know about you, but I'm going after her."

Just then Miya's SpaceBerry beeped.

WOOF, WOOF!
WOOF, WOOF!

SC Astron Girl
please report to the
FlyBy for mission
briefing.

Not now, she thought as she took it from her pocket.

Then she heard another SpaceBerry beep.

Honk! Honk!

"That's mine," said Olivia. "Let's go."

"I'm going to find Addie first," said Miya. "I'll see you there."

Miya raced out the pod's door, and as she did, she saw Valentina slip Olivia a note.

Outside, Addie was nowhere to be seen. Miya gave up looking and started making her way to the FlyBy. But first she sent Addie a message on her SpaceBerry.

ASTRON GIRL

Called to a mission. Forget about what just happened. Your party will be the best! C U soon. 🧸🧸🧸

CHAPTER ★ TWO

Miya was breathless from running when she reached the FlyBy's door. She quickly smiled into the security box on the door. The screen flashed.

"Welcome, SC Astron Girl," said Ms. Styles. "I've been waiting for you. Space Cadets Orbital 2 and Star Girl are here too. Now that we are all together, I can start the briefing."

"Sorry I was late, Ms. Styles," said Miya. She glanced at the other girls. Olivia was facing away from Addie, who had red eyes and a blotchy face. She looked back to her teacher. "Why are there three of us?" she asked. "Missions are always done in pairs."

"This time it's a little different," said Ms. Styles. "We think three cadets working together is what's needed to save this planet." She looked steadily at each of the girls in turn.

Addie stared at her feet. She knew Ms. Styles could tell she'd been crying.

"And the three of you look like you could use some time together to iron out a few problems."

"We're fine, Ms. Styles. Really," said Addie. "I just got a little upset about something, but I'm okay."

"I'm glad," said Ms. Styles, smiling. "It's not easy being away from your homes and families. The school tries hard to support its students. We make sure you have live video chats with family and friends. Special trips home on the school shuttle bus help too. But here in space we have to think of ourselves as another kind of family. We have to look out for each other. Isn't that right, Olivia?"

"Yes, Ms. Styles," she mumbled.

"Good. Now I'd like you each to sit down and take some time to learn about Rednessis. It's a nice little planet just at the edge of the super star cluster Gingela."

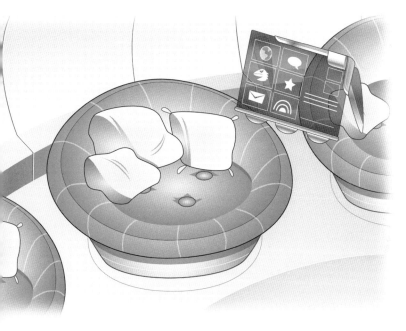

Addie looked at the clear computer screens floating beside five huge, comfy-looking round chairs. They were arranged side by side in a semicircle. The screens had icons running down the sides of them, but the screens looked like they were made of glass.

"These are so cool," said Addie.

"Yes, they do the job," Ms. Styles said, smiling. "While you girls are learning about the planet, I'll load myself onto your watches as the holographic teacher and check your GPS tracking chips. We need to know we can find you when you're on the mission."

Ms. Styles collected the watches and left the room. Addie jumped into the seat in the middle of the semicircle. Miya flopped down beside her, but Olivia left a chair between Addie and herself.

"Why don't you sit next to me?" asked
Miya.

"I'm okay here," answered Olivia. She
watched as Miya and Addie pulled their
screens toward them and touched an icon.
Then she quietly pulled out the note that
Valentina had given her and read it.

Come back with a bad mission
score and an invite to my party
is yours. V.

Olivia folded the note up and put it in her
pocket. Then she touched the SpaceChat icon
on her screen. Valentina was online.

ORBITAL 2

I'm not sure about a bad score.

SUPERNOVA

I'm first, Grace is second, and Miya is third on the scoreboard. I don't want Miya getting a good score. Don't you want to come to my party?

Olivia bit her lip. She glanced at Addie and Miya. They were talking and researching together. *Best buddies, roomies, and mission partners,* Olivia thought. *I'm always left out now. Besides, I'm last on the scoreboard. It won't matter much to me if we get a bad score.*

ORBITAL 2

Yep, I do want to come to your party. Thanks.

Olivia quickly closed the chat and then

touched the reptalien icon on her screen.

★ ★ ★ ★

When Ms. Styles returned she gave the girls their watches back. "Now follow me to Docking Bay 4," she said. "I'll brief you aboard the *Twin Rigger 1*."

Ms. Styles walked with Addie and Miya, and Olivia followed behind.

"I'm so glad you are on the spaceball team now, Addie. You have the makings of a fine goalie," said Ms. Styles.

"Thanks," said Addie. "I still have a long way to go, but I'm enjoying playing now."

They turned into the docking bay and stood facing what looked like two spacecraft stacked on top of each other.

"Do they fly together?" asked Addie.

"Yes," answered Ms. Styles. "Let's get aboard and I'll explain."

TWIN RIGGER 1

Small *Rigger* entry port

Small *Rigger*

Launch dec

Large *Rigger*

Quad rockets

Inside the cabin was a three-seat couch that curved around a table.

"Please take a seat, girls, and I'll quickly brief you," said Ms. Styles. "Rednessis, as you now know, is populated by blue, scaly reptaliens. They need full sunlight to function and stay healthy. Their tiny planet orbits around a yellow star a little like Earth's sun. However, their sun shines sunlight constantly on the area of the planet where the reptaliens live. But the planet has been plunged into darkness. We need you to find out why so that it can get its sunlight back."

"Do we need suits specially made for the conditions, like when we went to Planet Aquare?" asked Miya.

"Yes, we think it'd be best if you resemble the alien life forms of Rednessis," answered Ms. Styles. "You will find your spacesuits for this mission in the cabin lockers."

"What about our mission packs and any other equipment?" asked Olivia.

"Space Agent Cosmic Cruiser will take you through those and anything else you need to know during the flight. She will also fly you down to Rednessis in the smaller *Rigger.* We prefer that the larger *Rigger* doesn't try to land on the planet itself. It will hover a little farther away and wait for your return."

"Excuse me, Ms. Styles," said Addie. "Where's Space Agent Space Surfer?"

"SA Space Surfer is sick and in the school infirmary," answered Ms. Styles. "Just a bug. Okay, girls, it's time for me to leave you. Please work together and I trust you will have a successful mission."

CHAPTER ★ THREE

The doors of the *Twin Rigger* closed. A voice
Addie didn't know came through the cabin
speakers. "Welcome aboard the *Twin Rigger 1*,"
said SA Cosmic Cruiser. "We'll be taking off in
about ten minutes. Please put your spacesuits
on and prepare for takeoff."

Miya went over to the lockers and pulled
out the spacesuits. They looked like they were
made from shimmering scales in every shade
of blue. "It's scale-like fabric, not real scales,"
she said to the others.

"They have two tails on them!" Olivia laughed, taking hers.

"I'm almost too scared to ask what our helmets look like," said Addie.

"About the same," said Miya. "But check out the space boots!"

"Are those claws on the end of them?"

"Just over the toes," answered Miya.

The girls put on their suits and Miya let Cosmic Cruiser know that they were ready.

The *Twin Rigger's* rockets roared and it shot out of the docking bay into space.

★ ★ ★

"It's safe to move around the cabin now, space cadets," said Cosmic Cruiser. "Your mission packs are under your seats. You each have a flashlight and a packet of Rapid Repair.

Your flashlights have three settings for

different situations."

FLASHLIGHT AND RAPID REPAIR

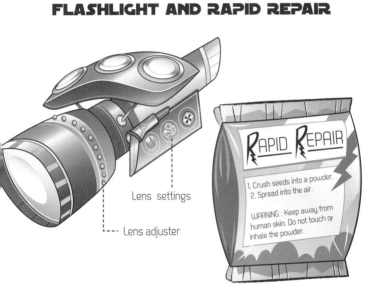

Lens settings

Lens adjuster

1. Crush seeds into a powder.
2. Spread into the air.

WARNING : Keep away from
human skin. Do not touch or
inhale the powder.

"The instructions for the Rapid Repair are

on the packets. There is also a D-Max Mag in

one of the storage bays. The D-Max is compact

when not in use. When expanded using the

Unpackit app on your SpaceBerries, it will pop out to the size of the cabin. The D-Max Mag has extreme magnifying powers."

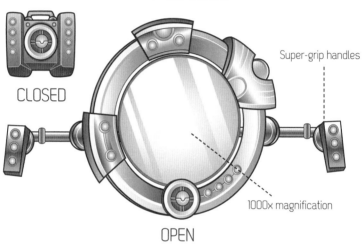

D-MAX MAG

CLOSED

Super-grip handles

1000x magnification

OPEN

"Doesn't magnifying something just make it seem bigger?" asked Olivia.

"Rednessis is tiny, so maybe everything on it is tiny, too," answered Addie.

Addie took out her flashlight and turned

it on. "The mirror setting doesn't really do much," she said. "But the kaleidoscope setting is great. Look at that!" The flashlight shined a spectacular pattern onto the cabin wall that moved and turned just like looking into a real kaleidoscope. "I wonder what we'd need these different light settings for?"

"Who knows," answered Olivia in a bored voice, and she began to take her flashlight apart.

"Why did you say what you said to Valentina back in the celebration pod?" Miya asked. It was the first chance she'd had to talk to Olivia about it with no teachers around.

"I think Valentina's party sounds better, that's all," answered Olivia.

"And you'd rather go to hers than mine?" Addie asked. *Please don't cry, Addie,* she thought. *Don't cry.* Olivia didn't answer.

Miya shrugged and shook her head. "Don't you like us anymore?"

"It's you two. Not me," Olivia snapped. "You leave me out all the time."

Miya's mouth fell open. She was about to say something when Cosmic Cruiser's voice came through the cabin speakers again. "We are about to enter Gingela. We'll be arriving in about fifteen minutes. Traveling through star clusters can get bumpy, so please store your mission packs and fasten your seat belts."

Addie and Miya repacked their mission packs and stowed them under their seats.

Olivia still had the lid of her flashlight off, and its power chip lay on the table. She quickly slipped the chip into the tissue she was holding and then put it in the trash. She packed everything away and the three girls sat in silence as the *Twin Rigger 1* flew bumpily through the gasses of the star cluster.

After a while the *Rigger* slowed. Then it seemed to come to a stop.

"Planet Rednessis is straight ahead, cadets," said Cosmic Cruiser as she came into the cabin. "You won't be able to see it yet. I've set the *Twin Rigger* to hover, and this is where we leave it. Grab your things and follow me. We'll be going down to the planet in the small *Rigger.* Awesome suits, by the way."

Addie laughed. "I'm sure looking like a reptalien must have its advantages or they wouldn't have made us dress like this!"

"Definitely," said Cosmic Cruiser.

When everyone was seated in the small *Rigger*, Cosmic Cruiser handed each of the cadets a set of night-vision goggles. "You'll need to attach these to your helmets," she said. "This normally sunny planet is in total darkness. I think you've used them before?"

GAS GOGGLES

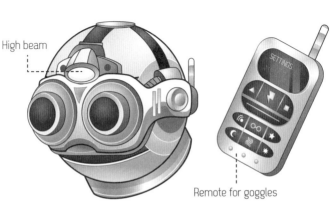

High beam

SETTINGS

Remote for goggles

"Yes, we have," said Miya as she took hers.

"Okay, does everyone have their seat belts fastened?" asked Cosmic Cruiser.

"Yes," the three cadets answered.

Cosmic Cruiser pushed the throttle and the small jet lifted off and then flew forward. Swirls of gas lit by several stars wooshed past the cockpit window. Then suddenly everything went black.

"We aren't in a black hole, are we?" Olivia asked, panicking.

"No," said Cosmic Cruiser. "We just entered Rednessis's orbit. If it's this dark here, it will be really dark down there." Cosmic Cruiser hit the hyper-lights button on the dashboard. "That's better."

The planet came into view.

"It's all red," said Olivia.

"Yes," said Cosmic Cruiser. "Didn't you learn that when you did your research?"

Olivia blushed. "Oh, I just forgot for a minute," she said.

"When it's covered in sunlight it's the most awesome shades of red," said Cosmic Cruiser. "I can't even see Rednessis's sun. Weird. Maybe the planet is between us and it, but I don't think it should be."

Cosmic Cruiser landed the small twin craft on a flat area of the planet. "Gear up, cadets," she said. "Your big moment has arrived. Good luck."

Addie and Miya adjusted their goggles

and put their helmets on. As Olivia went to get her helmet, she dropped her night vision goggles. She stepped back to pick them up and stood on them.

CRAAAACCK!

That should take care of them, she thought. "Oh no, I stepped on my goggles. They're broken. I'll have to stay here."

"No way," said Miya. "You know the rules. We both have night vision, so you'll be fine with us. Get your helmet on."

Olivia pulled on her helmet grudgingly and strapped on her mission pack.

Addie and Miya stood on either side of Olivia and held her hands.

Cosmic Cruiser hit the button and the door opened. The girls stood and looked out into total darkness. Addie and Miya switched on their goggles and the three of them stepped down onto Planet Rednessis.

CHAPTER ★ FOUR

The first thing the girls noticed was the noise.

Hiiiiiissss scrrreeeeeeech
CRAAAAAASH

"What's going on?" Olivia asked, gripping the other girls' hands tighter.

"We don't know," said Miya. "All we can see is rocks, cliffs, and crevices, and a few straggly plants. It's like being in the Grand Canyon. Why don't you see if your flashlight will help you see?"

Olivia's stomach turned over. *I wish I hadn't taken the power chip out of my flashlight just to wreck this mission,* she thought. *Or stepped on my night vision goggles.* She took her flashlight out and tried it. "It won't work," she said. "It must be broken."

Addie took her flashlight from her mission pack and gave it to Olivia. "Use mine," she said. "It must be scary not being able to see."

"Thanks," Olivia said as she took the flashlight and turned it on. The instant the light hit the ground all the noise stopped. Then a different rumbling noise started.

"What is that?" asked Olivia.

"Whatever it is, it's getting louder and louder," said Addie.

"Because it's heading for us!" yelled Miya. "Quick, turn the flashlight off."

Olivia did, and everything went still and quiet again. "I don't like this," she said. "I can't see and I'm scared. I want to go back."

"Shh," said Miya. "Listen. That other noise has started again, and it seems closer."

Hiiiiiissss scrrreeeeeeech

CRAAAAAASH Hiiiiiissss

"We need to go and see what it is. Without using the flashlight. Come on."

"No," said Olivia, shaking. "If I can't use the flashlight I'm not going."

"Here, have my goggles," said Addie, and she helped Olivia put them on. "Better?" she asked.

"Better, thanks," Olivia said with a small smile that Addie couldn't see. "But now *you* can't see."

"I've had a good look around, though," said Addie. "I'll be okay for now. We can share the goggles between us."

Suddenly there was a loud rumble and the ground shook underneath them. Olivia turned the flashlight on without thinking and pointed it in the direction of the noise. Creatures charged out of the darkness at them.

Olivia quickly shut off the light, but it was too late. The girls were surrounded by reptaliens, reptaliens that were attacking each other.

"What's happening?" Addie asked nervously. "It sounds awful."

"It looks like they're fighting each other, and they'll fight us too if we don't get out of here," Miya yelled.

Miya put Addie between herself and Olivia. The girls held hands and began to run back toward the *Rigger*.

"Aaagh!" Miya suddenly screamed. Then Addie was pulled to the ground and Olivia was jerked to a stop.

"What's wrong?" asked Olivia, turning back toward the others. Then she saw Miya on the ground holding her leg. "Quick, can you get up?"

"I can't. I slipped on something slimy and now my foot's stuck," Miya said. She grimaced as she tried to pull her foot free from a small gap between two rocks.

Olivia looked fearfully into the darkness, back the way they'd come. "I can still hear noises. We need to go," she said. She crouched beside Miya and tried to roll the smaller of the rocks away. It wouldn't budge.

"What are you doing?" Addie asked.

"Miya's foot is caught in a hole," Olivia said. "I can't get her out."

"Take her space boot off," Addie said.

Olivia helped Miya undo the top of her boot and her foot slid free.

With Olivia's help, Miya stood up but then cried out in pain. "I can't walk on my foot," she said. "It's my ankle. Here, take my goggles so you can see to help me back."

Addie put the goggles on. "Put your arms around our shoulders," she said to Miya. "We'll take most of your weight. We're almost there."

The three cadets reached the *Rigger* and hit the button for its doors to open.

"Quick," yelled Addie. "We need to shut the doors and stop them from getting inside."

The doors shut, and all that could be heard was the girls' breathing.

"Okay, there is no way I'm going out there again," Olivia said. "I was totally freaked out. I've never seen anything like that."

SA Cosmic Cruiser helped the girls get Miya into a seat.

Addie and Olivia were both worried about Miya.

"Do you think she's broken something?" asked Olivia.

"I'm not sure," said Cosmic Cruiser. "But

you girls check what's going on out there. I'll take care of Cadet Astron's ankle. There are a couple of ice packs in the fridge. She needs them on her ankle to stop the swelling."

Cosmic Cruiser left the girls and went into the small storage bay to get the ice packs. Addie and Olivia looked out the *Rigger's* window. All they could see were reptaliens fighting with each other.

"Why are they turning on each other like that?" Olivia asked.

"They need sunlight to keep them happy and healthy, remember?" Addie said. "Being in the dark must stress them out, so they do things they wouldn't normally do. That's why they were so drawn to the flashlight."

The girls watched a big reptalien lash out with its two tails, flinging smaller ones aside.

"That one must be *really* stressed out," Olivia commented.

"Have you been stressed out?" Addie asked her friend quietly. "Is that why you turned on me?"

"Oh, um, I'm sorry," Olivia mumbled.

"You know we're not trying to leave you out," said Miya.

"I've said and done some really dumb things, haven't I?" mumbled Olivia.

"Yep," answered Addie.

"It's just that you guys share a dorm room. You went on a mission together. You're even study buddies. You're always together."

Addie was quiet for a moment. Then she said, "What you did really hurt."

"I know. I'm sorry," said Olivia. "I was just feeling so left out . . ."

"I kind of know what you mean," said Addie. "If you and Miya were sharing a room and everything, I'd probably feel the same."

"We can talk on the way back to school," Miya said. "Right now we have to do something about this planet. You need to go back out there."

"I'm not going out there again," said Olivia.

"I have an idea," said Miya. "If we get the space blankets out and shine our flashlights on them using the mirror setting, we might be able to create a huge pool of light."

"And the reptaliens will all want to be in that light," said Addie as she pulled the big silver blankets from the drawer. "I like it!"

She laid one out over the plasma screen and selected the mirror setting on her flashlight. When the beam hit the space blanket, rays of light bounced off it and onto the floor.

"The reptaliens will love it," said Addie.

"Can you have two settings on the flashlight at once?" Miya asked. "Try the kaleidoscope one with the mirror one."

Addie tried it. Suddenly the whole cabin was filled with rays and patterns of light.

"Wow, it's pretty," said Olivia. "It's like

the disco ball in the celebration holopods.
Only here, there's so much more light."

"Come on, Olivia, let's do it," said Addie.

"I can't go out there again," said Olivia,
shuddering. She took off her goggles. "I don't
even want to watch anymore."

"I'll go on my own then," said Addie.

"But that's against the rules," said Olivia.

"I have to do something," Addie said. "I might as well take everything we've been given, just in case." She gathered up the Rapid Repair packs and stuffed them into her mission pack, even though she didn't know how they could help. Then she picked up Miya's flashlight and all the blankets and headed for the door.

"Wait," said Miya, and she took out her SpaceBerry and called Addie's number.

"Why are you calling me?" asked Addie.

"Answer and put your phone on speaker mode," said Miya. "If you're going out there alone, at least we'll be able to talk to you and help from in here."

"Good plan," said Addie as she set her phone to speaker.

"Hang on," said Olivia, looking very guilty. She scrambled around in the trash can by her seat until she found her flashlight's power chip. She put it back in the flashlight and handed it to Addie.

Addie and Miya stared at her.

"I'll tell you about it later," she said.

Addie didn't have time to ask any questions. She hit the button for the doors to open and out she went.

CHAPTER ★ FIVE

Outside, Addie worked quickly and quietly in the dark. She hung the space blankets over the wing of the *Rigger* and let them hang down like a curtain of silver. *Those reptaliens are so busy fighting that they haven't even noticed me,* thought Addie. *It's terrible what happens to them without sunlight. But they will love it when the flashlights turn on.*

Addie snuck over to a pile of rocks not far away. She checked that all three flashlights were set to mirror and kaleidoscope, then she balanced them on the rocks. *Here goes,* she thought and turned the three flashlights on.

A blaze of patterned light reflected off the space blankets and lit up the area in front of the *Rigger*. The reptaliens stopped what they were doing and charged into the light.

"What's happening?" asked Miya through the SpaceBerry.

"They're all in the light," said Addie. "They've gone quiet, as if they're sunbathing."

"No more fighting?" Miya asked.

"No. I think they're going to sleep," answered Addie. "Poor things. I'm going to take a look around."

"Keep talking so we know what's going on," said Miya.

"I can see a lot of those plants we saw when we only had night vision. There must have been tons before the sunlight disappeared because there are dead ones everywhere," said Addie. "That's what the slime was that you slipped on, Miya."

Suddenly Addie heard Cosmic Cruiser's voice through the SpaceBerry.

"Here's your ice pack, Astron. Hey, where's Star Girl?"

"Umm," said Miya, "she's outside."

"Outside?" came Cosmic Cruiser's shocked voice. "I'll have to contact Ms.—"

"Oh no, more reptaliens are coming!" said Addie, cutting her off.

HiiiiiiSSSSSSS HiiiiiiSSSSSSS

Hiiiiiissssssssss

"Can you hide anywhere?" asked Miya.

"I don't think I need to," said Addie. "They're heading for the light. They can see me better now, and I think they think I'm one of them."

"The reptalien spacesuits!" said Miya.

"Yep," said Addie. "But all these plants must have died from having no light. I'm going to use the Rapid Repair. Maybe it will help them grow when the planet gets its sunlight back."

Addie took out one of the packs. She crushed the seeds and blew the powder into the air. The effect was like magic. Wherever it landed the plants came back to life.

I wish I had more of this stuff, Addie thought. She crushed the next two packs and blew the powder around as she walked.

"I can't see anything strange," said Addie. "There's nothing out here but rocks, plants, and reptaliens. I'm going to call Ms. Styles."

"Okay," said Miya. "Be quick. We don't know how long those flashlight power chips are going to last."

Addie flipped her watch cover up. Ms. Styles appeared right away.

"SC Star Girl. What have you found?" asked Ms. Styles.

"Nothing, that's the problem," answered Addie.

"And you are out there alone. Cosmic Cruiser told me what's gone on so far."

"Oh, yes, but anyway . . ." Addie continued, trying to skim over the fact that she was breaking the school rules.

"No, Star Girl," said Ms. Styles. "Return to the small *Rigger* immediately. It seems like the problem isn't on the planet, anyway. I'll contact Cosmic Cruiser on the *Rigger's* communication screen and talk to her about this. Then I'll talk with you girls." And then she was gone.

Back inside the small *Rigger* the girls were listening to Ms. Styles on the rocket's screen.

"Sorry to hear about your ankle, Astron Girl. Hopefully it's only a sprain," said Ms. Styles. "And I hear you had a severe case of the spooks, Orbital 2. Don't feel bad. We've all felt like that at some time in our lives. I've instructed SA Cosmic Cruiser to orbit the planet. It seems strange that the sun can't be seen. Buckle up and we'll speak again later."

All three girls fastened their seat belts and the *Rigger's* rockets fired up. In no time they were back up in Rednessis's dark orbit.

"I'll be cruising slowly," said Cosmic Cruiser. "Yell out to me if you see or hear anything strange out there."

As the small *Rigger* flew across Rednessis's black sky, its light lit up a huge black shape.

"Is that something up ahead?" asked Addie.

"I'll go in closer," said Cosmic Cruiser.

Slowly, a massive black rectangular object came into view.

"What is that thing?" asked Addie.

"I think I know," said Cosmic Cruiser. "It reminds me of the energy filters used to collect and store sunlight. But this one is huge. I've never seen anything like it before. I bet if we fly in from behind it, we'll see Rednessis's sun. That thing is blocking the light from shining down onto Rednessis."

The *Rigger* flew around behind the massive screen and suddenly the rocket was bathed in brilliant sunlight.

"I think it's time to think about using the D-Max Mag," said Cosmic Cruiser.

"Of course," said Miya. "It can magnify the sun's rays, and if we focus the magnifying glass on the filter, the heat will cause it to combust and burn away to nothing."

"And then the tiny planet will have its sunlight back," said Olivia. "You and I can do this, Addie. We can use the safety cords and take the magnifying glass out into space."

"I'll fly as close as I can to where you will need to hold the glass," said Cosmic Cruiser. "Don't look at the glass or the filter screen. I'll tell you when the job is done through your helmet speakers."

The cadets attached themselves to the craft using the safety rope. Olivia took the little D-Max package and Addie made sure the Unpackit application was on her SpaceBerry's front screen. Then they went out into space through the *Rigger's* space hatch.

"It's just like when we play spaceball!" said Addie as they moved slowly through space.

"In position now," said Cosmic Cruiser's voice. "Hold the package between the two of you, hit the Unpackit app, and close your eyes."

The cadets held the package and Addie

hit the Unpackit app. Suddenly the girls were being pushed farther and farther apart.

The D-Max unpacked and unfolded into a huge magnifying glass. The girls held tightly to the handles and waited. Finally, they heard Cosmic Cruiser's voice again. "Open your eyes, space cadets, and look at your handiwork. Mission complete."

Addie and Olivia looked at where the screen had been. All they could see was beautiful sunlight, and it was shining all the way down onto Planet Rednessis.

CHAPTER ⭐ SIX

Back at the docking bay, the *Twin Rigger's* engines were cooling down and the crew was offloading from the main craft.

"Welcome home Space Cadets Star Girl, Astron, and Orbital 2," said Ms. Styles. "Onto the stretcher, Astron Girl, and then it's off to the infirmary for you," she said. "We'll all come up and visit you soon."

Two space station worker bots carried Miya away, and Addie and Olivia followed Ms. Styles into the FlyBy.

"Not a terrible mission, but certainly not one of the best," said Ms. Styles. "You deliberately broke your night vision goggles, Orbital 2. You wanted to get a bad score on this mission, I suspect. And you, Star Girl, went out on an alien planet alone."

"I had no choice," said Addie. "Astron Girl couldn't go and . . ."

"And if Orbital 2 wasn't up to going out either, then you should have stayed put and called in. You did have choices and you chose incorrectly, I'm afraid."

"Yes, Ms. Styles," said Addie. "I'm sorry. But I did manage to bring those plants back to life."

"Yes, you did," said Ms. Styles. "And you

and Orbital 2 did destroy the filter screen and sunlight is now falling back on Planet Rednessis. Still, I don't think you girls will score well. We'll soon find out."

Olivia looked at the ground. "May we go now, Ms. Styles?" she said.

"Yes. I can see you two girls have more to talk about," said Ms. Styles. "I hope this mission has helped you to understand each other a little better."

"It has," said Addie.

★ ★ ★ ★

Addie and Olivia sat on either side of Miya's bed in the infirmary. "Nothing's broken," said Miya. "I just have to stay off my ankle for a few days and see how it goes."

"That's good," said Olivia. "Look, I'm really, really sorry about trying to get a bad score out there. Valentina said if I made sure we didn't do well, I could go to her party."

"You'll get that invitation for sure then," said Addie. "I think we did pretty bad out there, but at least those poor reptaliens will be all right now. And I heard that Valentina and Sabrina did really well on their mission together. I wonder what the scoreboard will look like after today."

"I don't even want to go to Valentina's party now," said Olivia. "I've been pretty dumb lately. And you guys were so good to me out there. I'm sorry I got so scared and left you to do it alone, Addie, but I was honestly totally freaked out. I've never felt so scared."

"I know," said Addie. "I could tell you were. So what are you going to do now?"

"I'd like to go to your party, if I still can," said Olivia.

"I'd like that. Since Valentina's party is on the same night, though, it might just be the three of us!" Addie said. "And we'll try harder too, Olivia. It would be better if three girls could share a dorm room. Then none of us would feel left out."

Just then Grace walked in. "Hi, guys," she said. "I heard about what happened. How's your ankle, Miya?"

"Badly sprained," said Miya. "It will be better soon, though."

"Hey, Addie," said Grace. "I saw on SpaceChat that everyone you invited is going to your party. How cool is that? It'll be a really fun night!"

"Awesome," said Addie with a big grin. "Now I can't wait until Saturday night! I'm just going to go and say hi to Space Surfer. Do you know where he is?"

"He's in the isolation room," said Miya. "He's not allowed visitors. He has a vomiting bug and they don't want anyone to catch it."

"Oh, gross," said Addie. "Poor thing. I'll just send him a text then."

"Say hi from all of us," said Grace.

"Will do," said Addie, and she took out her SpaceBerry.

STAR GIRL
Hey, sorry you're sick. 😦

SPACE SURFER
Hi Star Girl! I'm feeling a little better.
I'm SO bored.

STAR GIRL
Glad you're feeling better.

SPACE SURFER
Yeah, I'll be back out there in no
time. What have you been up to?

STAR GIRL

I'm just back from a mission but we didn't
do very well. Missing our usual pilot. Ha ha!

SPACE SURFER

We can't win 'em all, Star Girl.
But we can try. 😊

SEAS HEAD OFFICE:
Your mission scores

Miya Wakuda: 4 points

Points deducted: 3 (new tally: 47)

Adelaide Banks: 4 points

Points deducted: 3 (new tally: 27)

Olivia Marston: 4 points

Points deducted: 3 (new tally: 25)

TOP TEN SPACE CADET SCOREBOARD

NAME	PHOTO	CADET POINTS	HOUSE
Valentina Adams (SC Supernova 1)		64	NEBULA
Sabrina Simcic (SC Neuron Star)		52	NEBULA
Grace Mauro (SC Comet XS)		50	NEBULA
Louisa Jeffries (SC Star Cluster)		48	NOVA
Miyako Wakuda (SC Astron Girl)		47	NOVA
Hannah Merrington (SC Galactic 6)		38	METEOR
Lara Walsh (SC Red Giant)		36	METEOR
Aziza Van De Walt (SC Asteroid)		35	NOVA
Samantha Winter (SC Shooting Star)		30	STELLAR
Adelaide Banks (SC Star Girl)		27	STELLAR

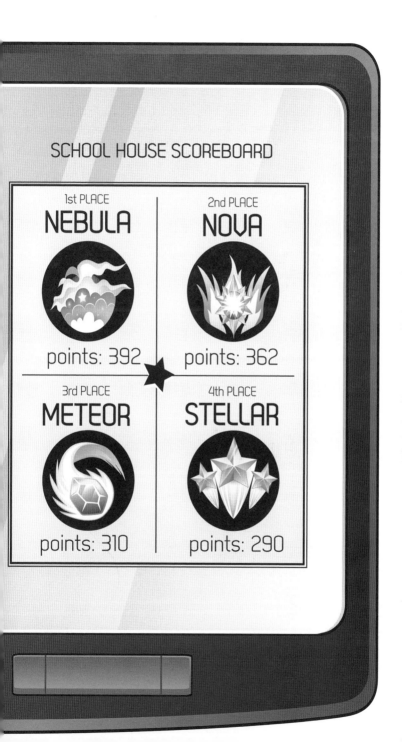

Check out all of Star Girl's space adventures!